P9-CLD-938

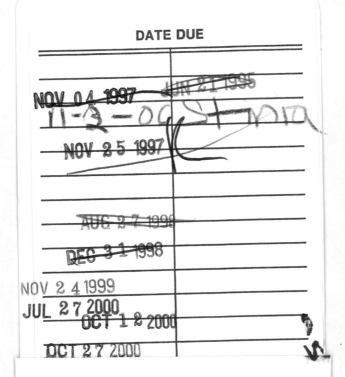

DATE DUE

NOV 04 1997   JUN 21 1998
11-3-00
NOV 25 1997
AUG 27 1998
DEC 31 1998
NOV 24 1999
JUL 27 2000
OCT 12 2000
OCT 27 2000

IDRAWN

NILES PUBLIC LIBRARY

Niles, Illinois

FINE SCHEDULE

Adult Materials . . . . 10 per day
Juvenile Materials . . . . . . 04 per day
Video Tapes . . . . . . $1.50 per day

WITHDRAWN

OCT 17 1988

I would like to dedicate the drawings in this book to you, Paul, with my love and thanks.

Ann

Text Copyright © 1980 by Roberta B. Rauch
Illustrations Copyright © 1980 by Ann Strugnell
All Rights Reserved
Addison-Wesley Publishing Company, Inc.
Reading, Massachusetts 01867
Printed in the United States of America
ABCDEFGHIJK-WZ-89876543210

Library of Congress Cataloging in Publication Data

Brown, Margaret Wise, 1910–1952.
  Once upon a time in a pigpen and three other stories.

  CONTENTS: Once upon a time in a pigpen. —Quiet in the wilderness. —A remarkable rabbit. —The gentle tiger.
  [1. Animals—Fiction. 2. Short stories] I. Strugnell, Ann. II. Title.
PZ7.B81630p3   [E]   77-5077
ISBN 0-201-00343-0

ONCE UPON A TIME IN A PIGPEN

A REMARKABLE RABBIT

QUIET IN THE WILDERNESS

THE GENTLE TIGER

ONCE
UPON A TIME
IN A PIGPEN

ONCE upon a time in a pigpen
There was a little pig who wouldn't eat.

7

No
He wouldn't gobble
He wouldn't snuffle
He wouldn't root
He wouldn't eat
Because he wasn't hungry.

"Have some slop," said his father.

"Have an orange peel sprinkled with coffee grounds," snorted his delicate Aunt Pig.

"You must eat your pigfood," snuffled his Grandmother. "Nice runny pigfood."

"Time to eat your slop," said his Mother. But the little pig wouldn't eat.

"Eat it quick or we'll eat it," squonked his piglet brothers from the bottom of the mire.

"Oink Oink Squiggle," squeaked his sister piglets rolling their little red eyes.

But the little pig wouldn't eat.

"Have some corn husks," rasped his uncle,
Old Uncle Pig.
It was such a good pig dinner that day,
Rotten turnips
Moldy potato peels
Dead cabbages
And lots and lots of runny slop.

But the little pig wouldn't eat. He just looked beyond his pigpen at the great green world beyond.

Now his Mother who loved him dearly, perhaps too much, was worried in her quiet pig heart. And she came creaking and whoofling over to him and whiffled in his ear, "What would you like to eat?"

"A bee, and some pine needles, and a red geranium — a nut, a fig, and a trillium — and a banana," said the little pig.

Now this was very difficult.

For how could the most loving pig Mother in the world find a bee, and some pine needles, and a red geranium — a nut, a fig, and a trillium — and a banana.

But she did.

Aunt Pig caught a bumblebee.

Father Pig went under the fence and picked a geranium.

Some pine needles blew by.

Old Uncle Pig dug up a nut.

A fig fell off a tree and none of the other pigs ate it.

And his own dear Mother brought him a trillium.

A banana peel just showed up.

And finally he gave a happy grunt; everything he wanted was before him.

"There you are," snorted his Mother.

And the little pig began to laugh.

"I was just fooling," he said. "I'm not hungry."

And for once upon a time in a pigpen this was the truth.

A
REMARKABLE
RABBIT

THIS is a Remarkable Rabbit. He thinks he will
run away.

From his Mother. His Mother is dreaming
about carrots and is not thinking about her
remarkable little rabbit.

This is the Remarkable Rabbit hopping

Away.

And this is the Remarkable Rabbit running
and jumping away.

But he falls into a deep dark hole.
In the hole are
    a frog
        a snake
            a worm
                and a porcupine.

The Remarkable Rabbit doesn't like them. But
they won't let him go home.
The frog sits on one foot
　　And the porcupine sits on the other foot
　　And the snake and the worm
　　　Tie him to a root.
Poor little rabbit. He can't hop. He can't run.
He can't jump. He can't get out of the deep
dark hole. But he can think.

He thinks fast.

Then he starts to sneeze.

"How come? How come? Jugarum, Jugarum. How come?" drums the frog.

"A mosquito just flew out of my nose," says the Remarkable Rabbit. "Kerchew!"

"Which way? Which way? Jugarum," drums the frog.

"Up," says the Remarkable Rabbit.

And the frog hops up and hops out of the hole into the air.

Then with his free foot the Remarkable Rabbit begins to scratch.

"What's the matter?" asks the porcupine, who is sitting on his other foot.

"So many flies hopping down the road," says the Remarkable Rabbit. "I itch."

"Which way? Which road? Which road? Which road?" squeaks the porcupine.

"Away up the road," says the Remarkable Rabbit.

And up waddles the porcupine, and waddles up out of the hole and down the road.

The Remarkable Rabbit begins to sniff and to squirm. And he sniffs and he squirms and jerks the paw the worm has tied.

"Why sniff? Why jerk?" wheedles the worm.

"Rotten cabbage," sniffs the Remarkable Rabbit.

"Which way? Where? Which way to squirm?" wheedles the worm who loves rotten cabbage.

"Up in the sun in a cabbage field," says the Remarkable Rabbit.

And the worm wriggles up and away.

Then the Remarkable Rabbit begins to shake.
And he shakes and he quakes and he wakes up
the snake. A snake can't make any noise. So the
Remarkable Rabbit keeps murmuring to himself,
"Big black snake lying in the sun, on a rock, up
the road in the sun."

Snakes love other snakes so the snake drops
the Remarkable Rabbit's other paw and off he
slithers.

And there is the Remarkable Rabbit alone
at last.

And does he sit there?

And wait for them to come back and catch
him again?

No indeed.

He jumps up and pops out of that hole so fast
you can hardly see little Remarkable Rabbit running down the road. And he runs and he runs
and he runs
       to his Mother.

"I'll never fall into a big black hole again,"
he says.

"Don't be silly," says his Mother. "You'll fall
into plenty of holes. Just remember that you can
always get yourself out of them. You are a Remarkable Rabbit. Never forget that."

33

QUIET
IN THE
WILDERNESS

A RABBIT lived in the wilderness
Far from the noises of machines and men,
Quiet of the sky
And the sun
And the moon
And the sea
And then

A crow cawed
The wind roared
A bird chirped
A bird sang
A bee buzzed
And the heavy wings of a gull
Beat slowly on the air
And everywhere
In the silence all around
The wind stirred
Grass and branch
And came roaring down the woods
And roared away.

A coot beat the waters of the sea
And a squirrel went off like a machine gun
And ran scratching up a tree
In the silence of nowhere.

In the silence over the sea
A fish jumped
The seaweed popped and the sand
sighed
In the low tide.
Even the clams broke the air
Squirting their clam holes everywhere
And the heron cried
Cac-cacophony above the tide
That swished on rocks
Where rustled by wind
The sea crept back and slowly in
And a crow cawed over a broken shell
That he dropped on the rocks
And that broke when it fell.

And bees buzzed
And the small mayflies
Made a terrible racket opening their eyes
Only the spider made no sound
As he spun diamond patterns
'Round in a net that caught the dew,
And the pear tree quietly bloomed and grew
While far off like a gentle song
The bell buoy rang its sea-slung gong
And a grasshopper whirred
And the night wind stirred
And the night fell down —
Not a sound.

Then the crickets began
And the owls and the frog
And the little birds cried in their sleep
And the dog gave tongue in his dream
And the rabbit ran into
A hollow log.

45

THE GENTLE TIGER

ONCE upon a time there was a very polite and gentle tiger in a world of extra polite and gentle tigers in the most civilized jungle in the world.

Now this little tiger had not always been polite; he had not always been gentle. He had entered the world growling and screaming with rage and pawing the air where his mother wasn't.

But he heard his mother roar at his father, "Grrrrrrr, if this little tiger doesn't learn to be more polite, the other little tigers will bite him, and the little tigers will fight him, and the monkeys will laugh at him in this, the most civilized jungle of the world."

Now a little tiger can bite and fight back, but no tiger can bear to be laughed at by a monkey. So the little tiger's growl grew softer and softer until he purred in a gentle purr — "purrrrrrr."

Then he sheathed his claws in his warm soft paws and waved them gently and foolishly in the air, and every tiger said, "What a gentle little tiger he is."

Now, there were lots and lots of tigers in this jungle, up in the trees and under the rocks and all over the place. Tigers everywhere. And if they hadn't been most polite, they would have eaten each other up and then there wouldn't have been any tigers anywhere.

So, after the first growl for what he wanted, the little tiger learned to say please. Please, when a tiger says it, sounds like a soft squeak — pleece!

The little tiger learned to give this short soft squeak, so pleasing to other tigers, when he was very young, and immediately all the other tigers gave him something to eat. Then his mother shook him by the scruff of the neck until he said, "Thank you," in a gentle rumbling roar — "Thaaaaaaaank Youuuuuuuu."
And then he slept when he couldn't eat any more.

The little tiger woke with a sneeze. And a monkey laughed, "Ha-ha! Quick," said his mother, "put your paw in front of your mouth when you sneeze or yawn, and sometimes when you laugh, or the monkey will make a monkey out of you."

Now monkeys have no manners. They never did have and maybe they never will. So, from then on the little tiger put his paw up before his mouth when he yawned, and put his paw up when he sneezed, and sometimes when he laughed. And he always closed his mouth to chew. And no monkey ever again got a chance to laugh at him for that.

And the little tiger grew older and stronger,
and stayed up at night longer and longer and
longer.

When the moon was full other little tigers came to play with our little tiger's bones. Our little tiger ran and jumped in front of his bones and pulled out his claws and waved them in the air. He showed the other little tigers his teeth. He had just opened his mouth to bite, his teeth flashing in the moonlight, when his father came bounding in.

"Stop! Stop, my tiger son," he said. "One bite and there will be a terrible fight, and all these little tigers will try to eat you up. Let the little tigers play with your bones, and then you can play with the little tigers and you will have many friends, in this the most civilized jungle of the world."

So, our little tiger let the other little tigers play with his bones. And they played with him too, and they were tiger friends. And at dawn a low gentle rumbling roar came from all the little tigers' throats, and they all ran home.

When the little tiger was old enough, he was sent to tiger school under a wild spreading black acacia tree.

As he set out for his first day at school, his mother said, "Don't growl until you are growled at. Keep your eyes open and speak when you are spoken to. Never forget that you are a tiger in this, the most civilized jungle in the world, and learn to get along with other tigers without fighting, and come home before dark, and pay no attention to the monkeys in the treetops or they will make a monkey out of you, and your tiger's dignity will be upset."

Under the big black acacia tree the tiger
teacher smiled a big toothy smile, and all the little
tigers showed their teeth as they smiled back.

"This first lesson," she said, "is called
'Pleasantry'."

"When do we learn to fight?" asked one of the
little tigers.

"Not until you have learned a tiger poem,"
she said.

"And what is a tiger poem?" asked all the little
tigers at once.

"I will groan it for you," said the tiger teacher.
  "Tigers wait a little longer,
  Till your little jaws are stronger."
Then she growled, "Our second lesson will be 'Howling at the Moon'."

Now, it was only afternoon and the sun slanted golden through the grasses right in the young tigers' eyes. And, of course, there was no moon, and so the little tigers wanted to roar "Nonsense" at her, but they didn't.

"Imagine the moon," howled the tiger teacher. "Keep imagining the moon," she moaned. Smiling her big toothy smile, she purred, "Imagine the moon high in a purple sky."

So all the little tigers lifted their little bewhiskered faces and howled at an imaginary moon.

First softly, then growling louder, the little tigers, prouder and prouder, howled. And all the little tigers howled and sang to that imaginary moon under the acacia tree all afternoon.

As our tiger padded home from school under the vine-hung trees in this, the most civilized jungle in the world, he heard the monkeys chattering in the treetops.

They talked loudly in high shrill chatter, all at once, and never listened to each other.

They ate with their mouths open.

They snatched things from each other.

And they sneezed and yawned in each other's faces.

They picked their teeth and their noses and their toes, as monkeys do, almost all at once.

They pushed each other off the branches of trees.

And pretended to have fleas when they didn't have fleas. And snatched and squabbled and never said please.

Monkeys!

The little tiger watched them for some time and then remembering that he was a tiger in this, the most civilized jungle in the world, he went quietly home.

For he was a gentle tiger and his dignity was never undone.

Margaret Wise Brown was born in 1910 and was educated in Lausanne, Switzerland; Dana Hall in Wellesley, Massachusetts, and Hollins College in Hollins, Virginia. She spent most of her life on Long Island, New York.

She first gained her wide knowledge of small children and the kind of books that evoke their spontaneous enthusiasm from the Writers Laboratory at the Bank Street Schools where she became a member of the Studies and Publications Department. Later, she became the first editor of Young Scott Books.

In an autobiographical essay, Margaret Wise Brown once wrote: "A book can accomplish something — to make a child laugh or feel clear and happy-headed as he follows a simple rhythm to its logical end, to jog him with the unexpected and comfort him with the familiar, and to lift him for a few moments from his own problems of shoe laces that won't tie and busy parents and mysterious clock time into the world of a bug or a bear or a bee or a boy living in the timeless world of story — that is if I've been lucky enough to write a book simple enough to do that or to come near to that timeless world."

Margaret Wise Brown died very suddenly in France in 1952 and is deeply mourned by the many who knew her and her work.

MARGARET WISE BROWN

NILES PUBLIC LIBRARY